Hailey Twitch

and the Campground Itch

Hailey Twitch by Lauren Barnholdt

- -

Hailey Twitch Is Not a Snitch

Hailey Twitch and
the Great Teacher Switch

Hailey Twitch

and the Campground Itch

Lauren Barnholdt
Pictures by Suzanne Beaky

sourcebooks
jabberwocky

Published by Sourcebooks Jabberwocky, an imprint of Sourcebooks, Inc.
P.O. Box 4410, Naperville, Illinois 60567-4410
(630) 961-3900
Fax: (630) 961-2168
www.jabberwockykids.com

Library of Congress Cataloging-in-Publication data is on file with the publisher.

Source of Production: Webcom, Toronto, Ontario, Canada.
Date of Production: March 2011
Run Number: 14825

Printed and bound in Canada.
WC 10 9 8 7 6 5 4 3 2 1

For Aaron

Contents

Chapter One

- - - - - - - - - - - - - - - - - - -

The Long Weekend

Bounce, bounce, bounce. That is the sound of me, Hailey Twitch, bouncing all around. And I am bouncing all around because it is a long weekend. Hello, long weekend! A long weekend is something that only comes along once in a while. It is when you get a Friday *and* a Monday off from school. It is like four whole days for the price of two. And that is some very good math.

This long weekend is going to be the best long weekend ever invented. And that is because we are going to Lake Missoni! Lake Missoni is very fun. These are the reasons:

1. We will sleep in a camper with a bed that pulls right out from the wall.

2. There is a swimming pool and a beach. That is two kinds of swimming!

3. There is a rec hall there with an ice-cream stand and an arcade and a basketball hoop.

4. My friend Addie Jokobeck is getting special permission from her parents to go with me.

Right now I am supposed to be packing up my clothes. I am supposed to be packing two swimming suits, two sweatshirts, three pairs of pajamas, and lots and lots of underwear. Plus, some socks and some shorts and some long pants. My magic sprite, Maybelle, is helping me.

"Now, Maybelle," I say. "Please go over there and bring me a pair of jeans out of my dresser."

Maybelle goes over to my dresser and tries to pull out those jeans. But it is very hard for her. That is because she is very small, about one foot tall! That is only the size of one ruler. Also, she has beautiful long blond hair and gorgeous sparkly wings, and I am the only one who can see her.

Maybelle used to live in my dollhouse. She got sent to live there because she was not a very good sprite. She was not fun like sprites should be. So Mr. Tuttle, who is in charge of the Department of Magic, made her live in there as a punishment. But she got to come out! And that is not even the best part! The best part is that Mr. Tuttle gave Maybelle her magic back. And now she gets to try it out for two whole weeks. That is called getting a new responsibility to see if you are ready for it.

So far I do not think Maybelle is ready for it. Yesterday we did a school play of *The Gingerbread Princess*, and Maybelle accidentally knocked over the whole gingerbread house. But that does not mean she should not keep trying. Practice makes perfect!

But before Maybelle can try some magic on packing my suitcase, there is a knock on my bedroom door. And it is my mom.

"Oh, hello," I say. "I am packing up just like you said." I run and get those jeans right out of my dresser. Then I roll, roll, roll them up and then stuff, stuff, stuff them into my suitcase.

"Hailey, you cannot stuff your jeans into a ball." She pulls them out of my suitcase and folds them nice and neat. And then my mom decides to tell me about something horrible. "Also, Maya Greenbert is coming to camp with us."

"I do not like this piece of news," I tell her. "And I am maybe about to have a good tantrum about it."

"Maya is Kaitlyn's friend," my mom says, "and so she is welcome to come camping with us. You are bringing a friend. You are bringing Addie Jokobeck." Kaitlyn is my sister. She is fourteen and thinks she is the boss of me.

"Yes," I say. "But Addie Jokobeck is nice and smart and has wonderful smooth hair, and she is not mean like Maya Greenbert." I think about maybe telling my mom about how one time Maya Greenbert would not let me share her bubblegum lip gloss. Maya Greenbert said that I would have too many germs on my lips since I am only in the second grade. But my lips were clean as a whistle!

"Hailey," my mom says. "Maya is not mean."

"Yes, she is," I whisper to Maybelle.

"What's so mean about her?" Maybelle whispers back real soft.

"I will tell you a story about some lip gloss later." I cannot tell her right now because my mom will hear me.

"Okay, Hailey," my mom says. She is looking into my suitcase to make sure I have everything all packed. My suitcase is red and says GOING TO

GRANDMA's on it. Which is not very fun or funny. But it is the only one I have. So I have to use it. Even though it does not make any sense since I am going to camp and not even going to my grandma's house. "Now I want you to fold these sweatshirts and put them in your suitcase," my mom says. "I am going downstairs to pack the food."

Once she is gone, Maybelle starts flying all around my head. "Tell me about Maya Greenbert, tell me about Maya Greenbert!" she says.

"Well," I say. "Maya Greenbert is a very big brat, and she—"

But then the doorbell rings. *Ding-dong.* "That," I say, "is probably her. So you can just see for your own self."

7

Chapter Two

- -

Maya Greenbert

Maya Greenbert is already being one big, big show-offy show-off.

"Look at my new suitcase," she tells me. "It is pink." She is standing right in the hallway outside my room. And she is shove, shove, shoving that suitcase right in my face.

"That is a very nice suitcase," I tell her, very polite. "But I am very busy packing now, so you should probably go to Kaitlyn's room."

"That is so cute," Maya says. "You are going to pack just like a big girl." Then she reaches out and pats me on the head. One, two, three times. *Pat, pat, pat.*

I feel myself starting to get mad, mad, mad. And that is because when someone tells you you are doing something just like a big girl, it really means they think you are a very big baby.

"Maya Greenbert," I say. "You better not call me a big girl again!" And then I stamp my foot very hard. And then Maybelle points her

wand right at Maya Greenbert's suitcase. But nothing happens. So Maybelle swoops right down and opens that suitcase right up. And all of Maya's clothes go tumbling all down to the floor. Even her underwear! And I cannot help it. I start to laugh. Because it is very funny.

"That," Maybelle says, "is what is called serving her right."

"Kaitlyn!" Maya yells. "Kaitlyn, get over here right now!" Maya Greenbert is screaming her head off for Kaitlyn. But Kaitlyn is not the boss of me.

"Kaitlyn," I say, "is not the boss of me."

"What is going on out here?" Kaitlyn asks.

"Hailey opened my suitcase and dropped all my clothes on the floor!" Maya says.

"No, I did not," I say. I am being very calm about all this. That is called keeping your cool.

But Kaitlyn does not get a chance to get upset. And that is because my mom is yelling from downstairs. "Girls!" she says. "It is time to go pick Addie up and then get on the road for camp!" And so Kaitlyn and Maya pick up all those clothes. And then they go downstairs.

"Maybelle," I say, "please finish folding my clothes with your magic."

And then Maybelle looks right at those clothes and points her magic wand. But they all turn into one jumbled mess. I sigh. I do not think she is really getting the hang of this magic thing.

- -

The car ride is very long. Three whole hours even! Here is how the seats go: my mom and dad in front. Kaitlyn and Maya in the middle seat. And me and Addie Jokobeck in the back. Sometimes I accidentally kick, kick, kick on Maya's seat with my purple sneakers. Maya does not like that too much. But she cannot prove it is me. Me and Addie Jokobeck eat some snacks, like one apple and one granola bar and four celery sticks with crunchy peanut butter.

When we get to camp, I jump out of the car because I cannot even take it anymore.

"Snakes!" I yell. "If you are anywhere around here, you better get away right now!"

"Snakes?" Addie Jokobeck says. She climbs down out of the van behind me. She is looking very scared in her face. Addie Jokobeck does not do too good with things that are scary.

"There are no snakes around here," Maya Greenbert says. She jumps out of the car and is looking very annoyed. She even gives her eyes a good roll. "Hailey is just using her imagination."

Maybelle gasps. That is because she does not like it when people say mean things about my imagination running wild. So Maybelle points her wand at Maya Greenbert's suitcase again. But nothing is happening. So finally Maybelle just swoops down and opens that suitcase right up. And Maya's clothes go flying all over onto the ground. Right into a mud puddle even.

"Oh, no!" Kaitlyn yells, jumping out of the car. "What happened?"

"Turns out that new pink suitcase is very much broken," I say. "Either that or Maya is just a little bit clumsy."

And then me and Addie Jokobeck go to check out the campsite.

Chapter Three

-- -- -- -- -- -- -- -- -- -- -- -- --

Magic at the Arcade

Our camper is very small. But also very perfect. There is one couch that turns into a bed for me and Addie Jokobeck. And two beds near the ceiling for Kaitlyn and Maya. And one big bedroom in the back for my mom and dad.

After we put all our things away, it is time to go to the rec hall! The rec hall is where you go when you want to play basketball. Or shuffleboard. Or when you want to play video games if you have some quarters.

My mom gives us each four quarters! But then she says me and Addie have to go to the rec hall with Kaitlyn and Maya only!

"But, Mom!" I say. "I am old enough to go by my own self! Addie is very responsible, right, Addie?" I look at Addie. Addie is very responsible. She always brushes her hair. And she knows how to print in very good, neat letters. And she always uses plain pencils without glitter or feathers. And she even won student of the month for responsibility.

"I don't know," Addie says. She is talking real quiet. She looks down at her hands. "I think maybe Kaitlyn and Maya should go with us."

"But we hate Maya!" I say before I can control myself. Controlling myself is not something I am very good at.

"Hailey!" my mom says. "That is not very nice! You know that we do not say things like that." My mom is unpacking a big box of plastic spoons and forks for later. That is when we are going to cook out on the grill and have very good delicious hamburgers oozing out with ketchup.

"I am very sorry," I say. "And since I have learned my lesson, Addie and I will be going up to the rec hall now, please."

"No," my mom says. "You will wait for Kaitlyn and Maya."

But Kaitlyn and Maya take about thirty bazillion hours to even get ready! They are giggling and laughing and talking about stupid boys, boys, boys. And they are putting lots of makeup on. Like sparkly lip gloss that makes their lips very red. And lots of stuff for their eyes that is very black and smooshy.

"Finally," I say when Kaitlyn and Maya come out of the camper.

We start to walk up to the rec hall. I am skip, skip, skipping I am so happy. "When we get there," I tell Addie. "I am going to play badminton and shuffleboard!"

"Badminton and shuffleboard?" Addie looks scared. "I have never played those before." Addie gets nervous when she thinks she has to learn some new sports. "Do not worry," I tell her. "You will not get hurt. Those sports are very easy, and you will love them!"

And that is when I spot it. Poison ivy on the side of the road! Poison ivy is a bad plant that makes you itch, itch, itchy if it gets on your skin. And you have to lie in bed for a long time, and it itches all on your skin, and you cannot even itch it, and if you do, you get very red. And your mom has to put special poison ivy lotion all over you, and you have to take lots and lots of baths in a bathtub that is filled with sticky, gummy, gooey oatmeal!

Maybelle is going right in the poison ivy! "Watch out!" I scream at her. "Stay out of that poison ivy!"

"What is poison ivy?" Maybelle asks. I guess they do not have poison ivy in that castle where she lived.

"Poison ivy is that plant right there, and it will get on your skin and make you very itchy, and it is not very fun or funny at all." Maybelle looks very scared. So does Addie Jokobeck. But Maya Greenbert thinks I am talking to her. And so she gets very snot, snot, snotty.

"I know what poison ivy is, Hailey," she says. "I am fourteen, not seven." Then she laughs.

I roll my eyes behind her back. And then I stick my tongue out right at her.

Maybelle is over on the side of the road, and she is pointing her wand at the poison ivy. "This poison ivy is going to be zapped right away!" she says. But her magic wand accidentally zaps that poison ivy so that there is even more of it! And poison ivy is growing all around and around and around.

I quick grab Addie Jokobeck's arm and

pull her away. "Watch out for the poison ivy, Addie!" I tell her.

But Maya Greenbert is not paying attention to where she is going. "Watch out for the poison ivy, Maya!" I say. But she is not listening to me. She is too busy talking about boys, boys, boys. So if she gets poison ivy, it will be all her own fault. Don't say I didn't warn her.

When we get up to the rec hall, I decide that it is time to play some video games in the arcade! Those quarters in my pocket are itch, itch, itching to be spent.

"Do you want to play video games?" I ask Addie Jokobeck. "We can play badminton and shuffleboard right after."

"Yes," Maya Greenbert says. "We are going to play in the arcade now. Come along, little girls."

I am about to yell at her and tell her that she is not the boss of me. And that she should not be calling us little girls. She is not even that much older than us! I am seven. And she is fourteen. And fourteen minus seven is seven! That is only seven years difference! I am not sure how many days that is because we have not learned to multiply that high yet. But it is not even long!

But before I can yell at Maya, I realize that Maybelle is over in the corner. And she is playing a video game!

I run right over to her.

"Maybelle!" I say. "Where did you get a quarter for that, please?"

My mom gave me eight quarters. Four for me and four for Addie. She did not give me any for Maybelle. That is because my mom does not know that Maybelle exists. And also because sprites should not be playing video games. Video games should be for humans only, thank you very much.

"I do not need quarters!" Maybelle yells. "I have magic!"

I think about this. Maybelle's magic has not been working so good. But maybe she got it working for video games because she is playing away on a driving game. She is a very

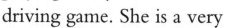

good driver, that sprite. I wonder if she had a car when she lived in the castle. But before I can ask Maybelle to maybe make some video games for me so that I do not have to spend my money on them, Maya Greenbert comes rushing right over.

She is twirling one of her very curly hairs around her finger. "Hailey," she says. "You cannot just run off like that. You need to let me and Kaitlyn know where you are at all times."

"Yeah," Kaitlyn says, running up behind her. "You should not run off like that. You are only a child." Gasp! That is not being a very good sister! Kaitlyn is very mean to me when Maya Greenbert is around. "Now we are going to stay in this arcade," Kaitlyn says. "And you and Addie are going to stay here, too. DO NOT LEAVE THIS ROOM."

"Don't worry," Addie Jokobeck says. "We will stay right in your sight." She does not realize that Kaitlyn and Maya are trying to be mean, mean, mean and boss, boss, bossy. But I decide to let it go. Letting it go is when you pretend you are okay with something when you are really not. But you just decide not to talk about it so that you do not have a fight or a big tantrum.

"Addie," I say. "Do you want to play this

game?" I bring her over to a very fun-looking game. It has a big claw. And you put in one quarter, and you could win a stuffed animal!

"I don't know," Addie Jokobeck says. "One time I heard my dad say that those machines are rip-offs."

"Oh, rips-offs," I say. "That is just what parents say when they do not want you to do something fun, fun, fun." Addie's dad Mr. Jokobeck is very nice. He lets us have food fights, and he does not even care when Mrs. Jokobeck says I am maybe a bad influence. But he is still a dad. And dads are very into the lies of something being a big rip-off. Rip-offs are when you spend some money on something that is not even worth it. Like if you use one of your quarters to try to win a stuffed animal, and it is set up so that you always, lose, lose, lose.

But I am feeling very lucky today! So I put

one quarter in the machine. Then I put that big claw right over this very wonderful stuffed dog with big brown floppy ears and a little black nose that is in there.

But then something horrible happens. Maybelle flies right up into the machine! And when the claw drops onto that dog, it grabs Maybelle instead.

"Ahhh!" she screams as the claw comes up and drops her into the chute. "Ahhh!"

"Oh my God!" I scream. "Maybelle, are you okay?" She pokes her head out of the door of the chute and looks out at me.

"Yes," she says. She sounds very grumbly. And very cranky.

Like maybe she is about to have a big fit or tantrum. Or maybe she hit her head when she got dropped.

"Well, you should not have been flying into a machine!" I say. "What is wrong with you?"

"Hailey," Addie Jokobeck says. She is looking around and seeming very confused. "Who are you talking to?"

"Um, no one," I say real quick. "Your turn!" I push her right up to the game.

Addie puts her quarter in, and Maybelle swoops out of that machine. Her hair is a very big mess. It looks like a rat's nest. That is what you call your hair when it is all tangly and even a good brushing won't get rid of all the knots, and you have to use a special spray that comes in a green bottle to get it back to being smooth.

"Everyone wants those stuffed animals," Maybelle says. "Because they are fun! I am going to get a stuffed animal for you and

Addie!" She takes out her sparkly wand. And she points it at the machine. I have a very bad feeling about this.

But when Addie puts the claw down, it grabs a stuffed animal!

"Addie!" I gasp. "You won!"

"I won!" Addie says. Her eyes are very big and round and shining. I do not think that Addie is used to winning things from video games. I am not used to it either. Of course she did not really win. Maybelle made her win. But still it is very wonderful and exciting!

"You won, you won, you won!" I scream. And then me and Addie are hugging and jumping around and doing what is called making a big scene. Some boys turn and stare at us.

"I cannot believe it!" Addie says. "I have never won anything in my whole entire life!"

We are screaming our heads off. And then

something very weird starts to happen. And that is that the claw machine starts to blink. All the lights on it are going craze, craze, crazy. They are going on, off, on, off, on, off. It is making me very dizzy in my head to look at it.

Maybelle says very quiet, "Uh-oh."

I do not like when Maybelle says "uh-oh." That is not a good sign. And then the claw machine starts moving. All by its own self! It is clawing up stuffed animals and dropping them down the chute very fast!

"Uh-oh," Addie says. "I think I broke that machine." She looks very nervous, like maybe she is going to get a big punishment for that.

"No, you didn't," I say. "That machine must have already been broken." I give Maybelle a very dirty look. That dirty look says, "Me and you are going to talk about this later, young lady."

"Hey!" a boy with red hair who is in the corner playing Skee-Ball says. "The machine is giving out free stuffed animals!"

And suddenly all the kids are rushing over to the machine and grabbing up stuffed animals. And I want to rush over there, too, and get some! Because it is not fair that all those kids are getting them! I should be getting them all. Since it is my sprite and her magic that have caused this big mess.

But before I can jump right in there, someone is putting a hand on my shoulder. And that someone is Kaitlyn.

"Hailey," she says. "We have to go."

"But there are free stuffed animals!" I say,

stamping my foot. Then that boy with red hair pushes against me very hard as he goes by to get those free toys.

"*Now*," Kaitlyn says. "It is an emergency."

And then I see Maya Greenbert. She is standing over by the door. And she is looking very miserable. And that is because she has itchy red bumps all over her legs.

Chapter Four

- -

Russian Spies

"I told you not to go in that poison ivy," I say to Maya. It is later that night. We are all sitting on logs around the bonfire at our campsite. And we are toasting marshmallows. I found a very good stick for toasting. It is long and perfect and skinny. I helped Addie Jokobeck find a good one, too. Hers is long with a good point on the end.

"That was not poison ivy," Maya Greenbert says. "I must have walked into it somewhere else." Maya Greenbert is covered all over in gross bumps. And red scratchy patches. And now she has poison ivy lotion all over her face and arms and legs. No one is wanting to go near her. That is because she is contagious.

"That was definitely poison ivy," Addie Jokobeck says. "'Leaves of three, let it be.'" That is a rhyme that we learned last year in Young Adventure Girls! That was a very fun group! I want to be in it again this year, but I do not know if I am allowed. That is because of a situation with some broken snowshoes from a field trip last year that was blamed on me for no good reason.

"What-*ever*," Maya Greenbert says. She is acting very grumbly. And also very snot, snot, snotty.

"Look at my marshmallow!" I say. "It is the most delicious marshmallow ever!" I take a big bite of that ooey-gooey marshmallow. And it gets all over my face. It is very delicious.

"Yum," Addie Jokobeck says. She takes a good bite of her marshmallow, too. But she is a very neat eater. It does not go all over her face.

"I do not know if I like marshmallows," Maybelle says. She is toasting her own marshmallow on a teeny-tiny little stick. Her hair is still a very big mess from that big disaster at the arcade earlier.

"Marshmallows are delicious," I say.

"Ewww," Maya Greenbert says. "You are making a mess of your marshmallow. But I guess that is what little seven-year-olds do."

"Yeah," Kaitlyn says. Kaitlyn is being very mean! And everyone knows that being messy does not have to do with how old you are. I have an uncle named Uncle James, and he is a very messy spaghetti eater and always gets tomato sauce all over his clothes. He is very old. Thirty-seven at least.

Then I see Maybelle get a little bit mad in her face. Her eyebrows go squoosh, squoosh, squooshing together. And then she pulls her wand out. And she points it at Maya's marshmallow! And suddenly Maya's marshmallow is an ooey, gooey, disgusting mess. It is going all over her hands and getting all in her poison ivy lotion, and it is very gross.

"Wow," I say. "You are making a very big mess of that marshmallow, Maya."

"Ahhh!" she screeches. "Kaitlyn, get me a napkin! Ahhh!" It is getting in her hair now. And all over her lips and face.

So Kaitlyn runs to get her a napkin. And Maya cleans herself all up.

"Well," I say. "I guess that some people are just not good with marshmallow messes. Some people who are fourteen and not just seven."

Addie Jokobeck is looking very nervous sitting on the log next to me. That is because she does not like fights too much. But this is not a fight. This is just two people talking about marshmallows and messy eating.

"Well," Maya says. "It doesn't matter about the marshmallows. Because tonight Kaitlyn and me are doing something that little kids cannot do. No. Matter. What."

And that is when I sit up and pay very close attention. And that is because when someone says "no matter what" that is when I get the most excited. Because that means it is going to be something fun, fun, fun.

"Me and Hailey are going to be playing Bananagrams in the camper tonight," Addie says. She does not know that this is a very bad plan. Bananagrams is very boring. It is like making up words with tiles for no reason. It is just a game that grown-ups try to make you do and pretend it is not like school. But it *is* just like school. And we are on a long weekend! And that means no school allowed.

"Hailey, Addie," my mom says. "It is time for bed."

"Okay," I say. I quick finish up the rest of my marshmallow. My mom looks very shocked, shocked, shocked. This is because I do not like going to bed usually. But tonight is not a normal night. And that is because I have a plan. And that plan is to sneak right out of bed and right out to see what Kaitlyn and Maya are up to! I need to find out what that "no matter what" plan is!

"Come on, Addie," I say. "It is time for bed." Addie does not know about our plan. So I do a real good yawn.

"Good night, Mr. and Mrs. Twitch," Addie says. Addie is very polite.

"Good night," I tell them. "I love you so much." I give them both kisses on their cheek.

"Don't forget to brush your teeth," my mom says. She is looking at me a little bit suspicious. That is because she knows I do not like doing all the things for bedtime like brushing teeth and hair.

"We are not really going to bed now, are we?" Maybelle asks. She is flying behind me and eating her marshmallow on a stick. It is very stick, stick, sticky. "Because that is not very fun. And I am hungry for lots more of these wonderful delicious marshmallows."

I do not say anything.

I just get into my pajamas with the glitter stars all over the pants. And Addie gets into her pajamas with the rocket ships and dogs. Rocket ships and dogs are a little tiny bit babyish to have on your pajamas. But I do not say that.

Me and Addie climb into bed in the camper. My mom and dad are still outside sitting near the fire. And Maya Greenbert and Kaitlyn are sitting at the picnic table out there.

"Now, Addie," I say. "I have a very fun

game for us to play. And that game is called
Russian Spies."

"Russian Spies?" Addie says. "Uh-oh." She
does not like when I have fun games for us to
play. That is because sometimes they involve
some things that turn out to be disasters. But
not this time!

"Yay!" Maybelle sings. "I want to be a
Russian spy! I love Russia, especially Siberia, it
gets very cold there in the winter."

I give her a look. And that looks says that
she does not know as much about Russia as
she thinks. Plus, I do not want to learn about
Russia. Russia is what you would learn about
in school. And I do not want to do schoolwork
right now, thank you very much.

"I don't think so," Addie Jokobeck says.
She is pulling out her green sleeping bag
and spreading it down on the mattress in the
camper. "I think we should just probably go

to sleep now." She gives me a smile and shows her two missing bottom teeth. "And then we can maybe play Russian Spies in the morning!"

"Russian spies do not work in the morning," I say. "They only work in the dark of the night." This is very true. Spies cannot just be running around in the day. They work when it is very dark, dark, dark. Usually I do not do so good in the dark. But in order to be a Russian spy, I will have to face my fears. That is what being a spy is all about.

"Now," I say. "I will wear this." I go into my suitcase. And I pull out one black sweatshirt. And one pair of black sweatpants. "What will you wear?" I ask Addie.

"I did not bring any black clothes," she says. "Plus, I think going out to play Russian Spies is against the rules."

"Yes, but," I say. "Russian spies are always breaking the rules. That is why they are spies."

Addie Jokobeck does not want to do this plan. I can tell. But I think maybe she just needs some convincing. So I say, "Maya and Kaitlyn are going somewhere. And they might get hurt! So we need to go after them and make sure they are okay."

Addie looks at me real serious. "Maybe we should tell your mom and dad," she says. She pokes her head up, up, up. And looks out the window to where my mom and dad are sitting on their lawn chairs. "Hey!" she yells. "Mr. and Mrs. Twitch, we have something to tell you that involves some safety issues!"

"Shhhh!" I say. I pull on her arm and take her back away from that window. "You cannot tell them! Then we will be tattletales! Do you want to be a tattletale?"

"No," Addie says. She shakes her head no, no, no.

"Okay, good," I say. "Now I wonder what we are going to do about you not having any black clothes." I raise my one eyebrow and give a look to Maybelle. And that look says to go and make some of Addie's clothes black. Using her magic. But Maybelle does not really notice.

And that is because she is working on making her own clothes black! She is giving herself a black T-shirt and black pants, and she is giving them sparkles all over! Which is not really fair when you think about it, since she knows that sparkles are one of my most fave, fave, favorite things in the whole world!

"I WONDER WHAT WE ARE GOING TO DO ABOUT YOU NOT HAVING

ANY BLACK CLOTHES," I say a lot more loud this time. Finally, Maybelle looks up from her own self.

"Oh!" she says. I take in a big breath and push it out in a sigh. Someone should really teach that sprite about not being so selfish.

Maybelle pulls out her wand. And she points it at Addie Jokobeck's suitcase.

"Now," I say to Addie. "Maybe you should look in your suitcase. There might be a black sweatshirt in there after all."

"No, there isn't," Addie says.

"Maybe there is."

"No, there isn't."

"Yes."

"No."

I take another big sigh. "Just. Check." So Addie does a big sigh back, and then she opens up her bag. And when Addie Jokobeck opens her suitcase, all her clothes come tum, tum, tumbling out! And it is a very big shock to her! Because all of her clothes are black. Black jeans. Black shirts. Black pajamas. Black underwear even!

"Oh my God!" Addie Jokobeck yells. "What happened to my clothes?!"

I look at Maybelle. "Sorry," she says and gives a shrug. "I guess I didn't know how to take control of my magic." She is looking at her wand very confused.

What a disaster of magic! "Well," I say to Addie. "You must have had some kind of a laundry accident." I know all about laundry accidents. That is because one time Kaitlyn washed her red school dress with my brand-new white costume of Little Bo Peep when it was almost time for Halloween. And that whole costume got ruined even. But I was not too mad because Little Bo Peep for a Halloween costume is not even that fun. What is fun is a witch. Or a vampire. Or a ghost with lots of drip, drip, drippy blood.

"A laundry accident?" Addie Jokobeck is looking like maybe she does not believe that.

"Yes," I say, patting her on the back. "Probably your dad tried to do the laundry. Dads doing laundry is always a very big disaster."

Addie Jokobeck looks like maybe she is going to cry. "Don't worry," I say. "We are going to be Russian spies, and that is going to cheer you right up!"

I give her another very big pat on the back. And then Addie Jokobeck and I change into our black clothes and head out of the camper.

Chapter Five

- - - - - - - - - - - - - - - -

A Very Big Amount of Trouble

I am very good at sneak, sneak, sneaking if I do say so myself. That is because I have had lots of practice in it. But Addie Jokobeck is not a very good sneaker. And neither is Maybelle. She keeps flying around and saying, "Russian Spies is very fun! Do you hear that, Mr. Tuttle?! I am being very bad and naughty by flying around and sneaking out!" It is a very good, lucky thing that no one can hear her.

"Come over here," I whisper to Addie. We sneak around to right behind the picnic table where Kaitlyn and Maya are sitting. They are looking through magazines and eating up the rest of their s'mores.

"What do we do now?" Addie asks.

"Now we wait for them to go somewhere," I say. I hope we do not have to wait that long. It is just a little bit cold out here. And my sweatshirt is not keeping me that warm. I pull the hood up over my head. But it does not really help.

But it turns out that we are very lucky! And that is because Kaitlyn and Maya tell my parents they are going for a walk! And they get right up! And start walking! This is not fair at all. My parents sent me right to bed. And they sent Kaitlyn and Maya right for a walk!

"Come on," I whisper. I put a finger to my lips, and we start to creep, creep, creep right after Kaitlyn and Maya. Addie looks very nervous about all this. But she really should not be so scared. Because there is no reason to be nervous. She needs to get used to breaking the rules more. And I am just the girl to help her with that.

Then I step on a branch. *CRACK!* We both stop right in our tracks. I am expecting to hear my parents say, "Hailey, is that you? Get back here this instant!" But I do not hear anything. So I keep going.

We follow Maya and Kaitlyn down the dirt

road. We follow them back into the bushes. We follow them a little bit into the woods.

"It is supposed to be right here," we hear Kaitlyn say. "It should be up in one of these trees."

"I don't see anything," Maya says.

"What are they talking about?" I whisper to Addie. It is very cold out here. And pitch-black and dark. I cannot see a thing. Not even right in front of my face! Next time we play Russian Spies we will have to steal my dad's flashlight for definite.

"I don't know," Addie says. "Maybe we should go back to the camp."

"No!" I say. "That would be being a quitter!" Being a quitter is not very good. It is what you do when you give up. And we have to find out what Kaitlyn and Maya are talking about that is up in one of those trees!

"But, Hailey—"

"I will make you see!" Maybelle yells. And

before I can stop her, she is moving her wand all around. And she shoots a light out of it! And it is lighting up the whole woods even! Like a big huge sparkler!

"No, Maybelle!" I say. "Stop that!"

"Maybelle?" Addie asks. "Who is Maybelle?"

"What's going on?" Maya Greenbert asks. "Who is that? Who's there?"

And then Kaitlyn and Maya are running right back to where we are standing. "Hailey!" Kaitlyn yells. "You are supposed to be in bed! Mom and Dad are going to be really, really mad at you!" She is putting her hands on her hips she is so mad.

"Oh, hello," I say. "Nice night for a walk, isn't it?" I quick give her a smile and try to make friends.

But Kaitlyn and Maya do not want to make friends. And so they march us right back to camp.

- -

I am in a very big amount of trouble. Because I am not supposed to be sneaking out of the camper. My mom and dad are going to give me a good punishment. They have just not decided on what yet. Probably I am going to get that punishment when we get home. On account of them not being able to punish me when I have Addie Jokobeck at camp with me. They tell me all of this bad news. And then they send me and Addie right back to bed.

So the next morning I am not in a very good mood, thank you very much.

"Maybelle," I grumble as I walk to the

shower building. "You should not have done that! Putting up a big light in the sky!"

"I did not know that was going to happen!" she says. "I thought it would only be a little bit of a light! And that only you would be able to see it!"

"Yes, well, you do not have a very good hold on your magic! You need to do some homework on it or something." Homework is what you do when you are trying to get better at something. It is like practice. "Maybe I will talk to Mr. Tuttle about some magic homework for you to work on."

"But I am really trying!" Maybelle says. "Cross my heart and promise!"

"I do not know if that is true, Maybelle Sinclair," I say. "I am really trying" is what I say when I get in trouble. And I am not always trying too hard, if you want to know the whole truth and nothing but the truth.

When we get to the shower building, Maya Greenbert is running up behind me. She is very out of breath and very itchy and red from her poison ivy. I make sure I do not get too close to her.

"Hailey!" she says. "Your mom sent me to walk you here, since you are not allowed to be walking around camp all by yourself."

"You are not the boss of me, Maya Greenbert!" I say.

"Hailey!" Maybelle says. "That is not very good manners."

But Maya Greenbert does not even yell back at me! And that is because she has other things on her mind. "Who were you talking to?" she asks. She is looking around all suspicious.

"What do you mean?" I try to sound very innocent like I do not know what she is talking about not even one little bit. I blink my eyes at her like she is being very confusing.

"I just heard you talking to someone," she says. She puts her hands on her hips. That is what people do when they are trying to boss you. "You told them they do not have a very good hold on their magic."

"I did not," I say.

"Yes, you did."

"No, I didn't."

"Yes, you did!" she says. And then she gets a big smile on her face. "Oh, I see," she says. "You have an imaginary friend." She gives me a pat on the head. "That is very cute."

Maybelle gets very mad about that. She flies right up and yells into Maya Greenbert's ear. "I AM NOT IMAGINARY!"

But Maya Greenbert cannot hear her, of course.

So she does not say anything back.

And then Maybelle flies into the shower cabin. I do not know what she is doing in there.

But something tells me it is not very good. I decide that I will not fight with Maya Greenbert. I am in enough trouble already. So I just go right by her and into the cabin.

Maybelle does not show up all through my shower. She does not show up when I shampoo up my hair. She does not show up when I get dressed in my most favorite pair of purple shorts and my most favorite shirt with the sparkly pink heart on it. She does not show up when I am done brushing my hair and putting in a beautiful glittery bobby pin that makes me look just like a movie star. She does not show up when I am posing right in front of the mirror, pretending I am famous.

And neither does Maya Greenbert. She is taking a very long time in that shower. Just like Kaitlyn does. That is what teenagers do. It is called being very annoying. So finally I gather up my shower caddy and head right back to the camper.

Everyone is there having a nice big breakfast at the picnic table.

"Hailey!" my mom says when she sees me. "Where is Maya?"

"She is still in the shower." I take a big shrug and sit down next to Addie Jokobeck. Addie already had her shower before me. Her hair is very perfect and dry and smooth.

"Hello, Addie," I say. "And how are you this fine morning?"

"Good," she says. She giggles. There is a big plate of delicious-looking waffles sitting in the middle of the table. So I take one and put it on my plate. Then I squeeze a very lot of syrup all over it.

"Hailey!" my mom says. "You know you

are not allowed to be walking back from the shower cabin by yourself. You were supposed to wait for Maya to walk back with you!"

"I *was* waiting!" I say. "I was waiting and waiting and waiting forever, but she did not come, not even after fifteen whole minutes." I do not really know if it was fifteen whole minutes. I do not have a watch. Also, I am not so good with clocks that have hands.

"Hailey, you know the rules," my mom says. "I cannot believe you are misbehaving so much!"

But before she can even say anything else, we hear a big noise. And that big noise is Maya Greenbert. She is running down to the camper with a big towel on her head, scream, scream, screaming. Louder than anything I've ever heard even.

"What's wrong?" Kaitlyn asks. "Why are you screaming like that?"

And then Maya Greenbert takes that towel off her head. Kaitlyn gasps. I gasp. Addie gasps. My mom and my dad gasp. Maybelle pops up and just says, "Oops."

Because Maya's hair is green. Green, green, green like a turtle.

"Wow," I say. "I think that is a very good

look for you, Maya." I take a big bite of syrupy waffle. But Maya Greenbert is very mad.

"You!" she says. And she points at me. "You did this to my hair!"

"Me?" I put a very shocked look on my face. "I could not do that to your hair. I am only seven. And people who are only seven do not know how to give other people green hair!" Which is very true.

"I did not mean it," Maybelle says. "I was trying to make her shampoo so that it would get bub, bub, bubbly, and she would have to spend a long time washing it out. But I do not think I did it right." She looks down at her wand with a very sad face.

"Okay, Maya," my mom says. "Calm down. I am sure it's just something that happened with your shampoo. Go and get the bottle, and we'll see if we can call the company who makes it."

Addie Jokobeck is looking at me. So is

Kaitlyn. But I did not do it. And they cannot prove it. So I just say, "Kaitlyn, would you like some syrup?" And then I enjoy the rest of that wonderful breakfast.

Chapter Six

Mr. Tuttle

After breakfast, my dad takes me and Addie
Jokobeck to the beach. That is because my
mom and Kaitlyn and Maya are still working
on her hair problem. They are driving her to
the hairdressing shop down the road. So that
she can get her hair all dyed up. I do not like
going to the hairdressing shop. That is because
the ladies there always cut your hair all off and
yank it with a brush. Then they tell you you
should do a much better job of brushing your
hair every day. That is called being lectured.
And it is not very fun or funny.

I am wearing my new blue and purple

bathing suit. And Addie is wearing her bathing suit that used to be green but is now black. Yikes.

Maybelle is not wearing any bathing suit. She is wearing a yellow dress. That is because she is scared of the water. She said that sprites do not like to go swimming. I tried to tell her there is nothing to be scared of. But she did not want to listen. So she is over sitting in the sand. And she is looking very grump, grump, grumpy.

My dad is sitting on the sand, too. He is reading a book and looking very grumpy just like Maybelle. That is because he is supposed to be golfing right now with his very best friend Ted. But he could not go. On account of the fact that he had to take us to the beach. On account of the fact that my mom had to take Maya and Kaitlyn to get Maya's hair fixed. On account of her green hair.

I think she should have just kept that

beautiful green hair. It was very special and different. But no one would listen to me.

"Now," I say to Addie when we are in the lake. "You and me are going to play sharks." I put my hand up in the water. "I am a shark and that is my fin, and I am going to get you."

Addie shrieks and tries to splash me. But you cannot just splash a shark away. It does not work like that.

"I am a shark!" I say again. And I grab Addie's leg in the water. "And you are my dinner!"

I wait for Addie Jokobeck to scream very loud. She does not like to be startled. But when it does not happen, I look up. And that is because I did not grab Addie Jokobeck's leg! I grabbed someone else's. A boy!

This is horrible since I do not like strangers. And I do not like boys. This weird boy is giving me a very big smile. He is missing all his top and bottom teeth, and he has five whole freckles on his nose. And then I recognize him immediately right away! He is the red-haired boy who pushed me right out of the way in the arcade! He ran up and stole that stuffed dog that I really wanted.

"Sorry, Boy," I say. "I thought you were my friend Addie Jokobeck." I turn around to look for Addie. And there she is, splashing over in the water away from me.

"Addie!" I yell. "We are supposed to be playing shark. Remember?"

"Yes," she says. "You were going to be a shark and find me and eat my brains."

"Right!" I say. "Because your ship has overturned, and you are lost at sea and a big pirate was after you, but now you are maybe going to get eaten right up by a shark."

I go to swim underwater. I am very good at underwater swimming. You just blow water right out of your nose and keep your eyes shut very, very tight, and it is very easy and fun.

But before I can go into that nice cool water, someone is tapping me on the shoulder. I turn around. It is that boy!

"Boy," I say. "Please go away."

"My name is not Boy," he says. And he gives me a big grin. "My name is Hayden, and I am eight, and I have seen a shark in real life."

I do not want to listen to this. But I have to admit that I am very interested in someone who has seen a shark in real life.

"You saw it in this water?!" Addie Jokobeck yells. She is looking like maybe she wants to run right out of this place. "I told you it was too cold to go swimming, Hailey!"

"No," Hayden the Stranger Boy says. "I did not see it here. I saw it in North Carolina. That's where my grandma lives."

"Did that shark bite you?" I ask him. I look at his arms to see if there are any huge teeth marks.

"No," he says.

"Did you get a picture of it?"

"No."

"Was it a big story on the news?"

"No."

"Then you are a liar."

"I am not a liar!" he says. But I do not believe him. Because "I am not a liar" is what I say when I am lying about something.

"Come on, Addie," I say. "That boy we just met is a big fat liar." We swim away, and then

Maybelle flies over and gives that boy a little paddle of water with her wings. And it goes right into his face. I want to laugh. But I do not. Because it is not that good to get water right in your face. It happened to me at a pool party once, and I did not like it one little bit.

"Wait!" the boy says. He is swimming very fast behind us. I just ignore him. But then he says, "Aren't you the girl who made that arcade game go crazy and give everyone stuffed animals?"

I stop swimming right away.

"Maybe," I say. "Why do you want to know?"

"Yeah," Addie says. "Why are you asking her that?" She comes over and stands really close to me in the water. That is what is called being one very true friend.

"I am asking," the boy says, "because you are very famous."

"Famous!" I say.

"Famous!" Maybelle says.

71

"Famous?" Addie Jokobeck asks.

"Yes," the boy says. "You are very famous, and everyone is still talking about it."

"Yes, well, it was me," I say. "My name is Hailey Twitch, and I do not give autographs." I have never been famous before! I wonder if they are going to put my picture in a magazine or in the newspaper or on an Internet website! Or hang it on the wall in the arcade. Maybe I will get some kind of prize or award. Like a million dollars even! Or maybe they will—

"Hailey Twitch!" someone yells from the beach. It is probably one of my fans. Fans are what you have when you get to be very famous. They are people who love your work. I will just have to tell that fan that I am very busy and I do not give autographs, thank you very much.

But when I turn around, it is not a fan! It is Mr. Tuttle! Mr. Tuttle, who runs the Department of Magic, and who gave Maybelle two weeks to get her magic under control! But it has not been two weeks yet. I know this because I am very good with days. That is because I have a very special Velcro calendar that shows all the days and even has a good place for weather.

"Hailey Twitch!" he says again. He is standing on the beach and waving his arms all around like he is craze, craze, crazy. I am starting to get very nervous in my stomach. I do not know what to do. Addie Jokobeck is right there with that boy Hayden!

"Um, excuse me, please," I say to Addie and

Hayden. "Excuse me, please" is a very polite thing to say and is good for when you want to use your manners. "I will be right back."

I run right up on the beach. "Hailey!" Mr. Tuttle is yelling. He is trying to run after me. But he is having a hard time. That is because he has a very big belly. I do not think he is in very good shape. He probably needs to do a few exercise classes like the way my mom does.

"Hailey!" Mr. Tuttle says. He is huffing and puffing up behind me. "Please do not run away from me! It is very rude and not good manners."

I want to tell him that being very rude and not using good manners is showing right up when someone is having a very fun game of shark with their very best friend Addie Jokobeck and also learning all about how they are famous. But I do not say that. Because I do not want to upset Maybelle.

She is flying all around my head and is getting very nervous. Maybelle is very afraid of Mr. Tuttle. She thinks he is worse than a principal even.

I sit down on the beach and pretend to be making a sand castle just in case my dad looks right over here. And Maybelle sits down right next to me. Her face is getting very splotch, splotch, splotchy like she is going to start crying any minute even. "Maybelle," I say. "You better get it together."

Mr. Tuttle pulls out his clipboard.

"Now," he says, "as you know, I have given Maybelle two weeks to practice her magic."

"Right," I say. I am trying to maybe sneak a look at his clipboard. I need to know what he is writing on there! I am looking right out of the corner of my eye very sneaky like. That is the way this boy Randall in my class does it when he is trying to look and copy answers off other people's spelling tests.

"That is fourteen days," Mr. Tuttle tells me.

"I know how long two weeks is," I say. "I am in the second grade, remember?" We have learned all of that stuff forever ago about days and months and years even.

Mr. Tuttle stands up very straight, straight, straight. His big brown shoes are sinking right into the sand. "So far Maybelle has changed your socks into two different colors, knocked down the gingerbread house in the play *The Gingerbread Princess*, made some poison ivy appear, and turned a girl named Maya Greenbert's hair green." He looks at me over his glasses. "Is this true?"

"Um, well…" I look at Maybelle. I think about maybe telling a little fib. But I know that I cannot lie to Mr. Tuttle. He is the head of the Department of Magic. And so he knows everything. He really is just like a principal. So I say, "Yes, that is true."

"But I was not trying to do any of those things!" Maybelle says. Now she is sitting right on my lap. She is very, very nervous. "It was an accident."

"Yes," I say. "It is very true that she did not do any of those things on purpose." I quick give Mr. Tuttle a big smile. "So you can give her some more time with her magic. Now if we're all done here, I am in the middle of a very good game of shark." I am getting very nervous to get back to that game. And that is because I can see Addie Jokobeck talking to that boy Hayden. They might even be becoming best friends without me.

"No," Mr. Tuttle says. He gives a big frown, and his forehead gets lots and lots of wrinkles in it, just like the old man who lives across the street from me, Edgar Frisk. I think Mr. Tuttle might be very old. Forty-nine, at least. "It seems like Maybelle is having a very hard time getting her magic under control. I am very sorry, but I think I am going to have to take it away."

"What?!" Maybelle screams. "No, no, no, no, no!!" She zooms all around.

"NO!" I yell. I stand up and shake my finger right at him. "Mr. Tuttle, that is not very nice!" A few people walking by on the beach turn to look at me. They think I am maybe very nutso in my head.

"Please," Mr. Tuttle says. "You must both stop having tantrums. That was the deal we had."

"But you said two weeks!" I screech. "And it has not been two weeks. It has only been about twelve days!"

Mr. Tuttle sighs. He looks back down at his clipboard. I hold my breath very tight. And so does Maybelle. And then Mr. Tuttle says, "All right. Fine. I will give Maybelle one more chance. But if she does not do something very good with her magic, then she will have to get it taken away. *Immediately.*"

And then there is a flash of blue lightning, and Mr. Tuttle is gone!

Maybelle falls right down into the sand. And

she is crying. Very much crying, like I do when I am very, very upset about something that is very, very important.

"It is okay," I say. I rub her back so that maybe she will feel better. Then I take part of my towel and dip it into the lake water. I put it on her forehead to try and make her feel calm, calm, calm. That is what my mom always does when I am feeling very sick.

"Do you feel calm from this towel on your head?" I ask her.

"No," she says. "I feel very wet and dripping."

"Hmm," I say. That lake water is getting all in her hair. Usually when my mom does this she uses a nice washcloth. And some very warm water from the sink. But there are no washcloths or sinks on the beach. And then Maybelle goes flying up into the air. She is dripping water everywhere!

"Please be careful, young lady," I tell her. "You are dripping water all over my legs."

"I do not care," she says. "I am not allowed to have my magic back. I am a huge disaster with magic!" She sits back down on the sand and covers up her face with her beautiful sparkly wings.

"Maybelle," I say. "You are not a huge disaster with magic." That is called telling a very small lie so that you can make someone feel very better. Because if you want to know the whole truth and nothing but the truth, Maybelle is a very big disaster with her magic. Even more of a disaster than I am with not having tantrums.

"Yes, I am!" she says from under that wing.

"Maybelle," I say. "It is time to look on the

bright side! You have one more chance! And one more chance is all you need!" I am very good at making the most of one more chance. One time I had one more chance to be good so that my dad would not have to take away all my TV time. And I did it.

"Yes, but Mr. Tuttle says it has to be something good," she says.

"Maybelle," I say. "Do not look so upset. We will figure it out."

She looks up at me with her poor crying face. "We will?"

"Yes!" I say. "I will help you, do not worry. Because that is what friends do."

Chapter Seven

A Disaster Area of a Tree House

When I get back in that water, Addie Jokobeck is talking to Hayden. They are talking away like they are having a very good time without me. I am feeling myself starting to get very, very jealous. I do not want Addie Jokobeck to be best friends with Hayden. She is best friends with me! Plus, I am in a very worried mood about Maybelle and her magic.

"What is going on over here?" I ask Addie. "Why are you talking to him?"

"He is telling me something very important," Addie says.

"Also, I am taking your turn at being a

shark," Hayden says. "And I won."

I make my eyes go very small, small, small. And that is so Hayden knows that I do not want to be messed with, thank you very much. "That is not very nice," I say. "To take someone's turn. That is horrible manners." I look at him. "What grade are you in, please?"

"Third," he says.

"Well, if you are really in third grade, then you should know that to take someone's turn is horrible, horrible, bad manners." I shake my finger at him. Taking turns is something you learn in kindergarten even. I am very good at taking turns if I do say so myself.

"Well, you were being very slow up on the beach," he says. "What were you doing up there anyway?"

"That is none of your business," I say. Then I stick my nose right up in the air. "Come on, Addie."

"But I am not done playing shark," Addie says, looking very sad.

"That is just too bad," I say.

"Wait!" Hayden says. He is swimming after us. But I am not in the mood. So I just take Addie's hand and walk right out of the water and onto the beach.

"I have a good secret to tell you," Hayden says.

I stop. My one true weakness is secrets!

"What kind of secret?" I ask. I drop Addie's hand and turn around.

"A secret about a disaster area," he says. And then he wiggles his eyebrows up, up, up, and down, down, down.

"I do not need to know any secrets about disaster areas," I say. "Disaster areas are boring, and I already know about a lot of them." This is a very true statement. One time I made a disaster area out of our whole kitchen by trying to make French toast in the toaster. And Kaitlyn's whole room is a very huge disaster area all of the time. So I do not need to know about those. I grab Addie's hand again and start to pull her away and right up onto the sand.

"Wait!" Hayden says. "This one is a disaster area of a tree house."

"A tree house?" I stop right in my tracks. I love hearing about tree houses! It is my one true dream to have one of my very own. Also, the meanest girl in room four, Natalie Brice, has a tree house with a pink door and a window that sees right up to the sky, and she is very bossy about it.

"Yes," he says. "It is in the woods, and if you meet me here tomorrow I will show it to you."

And then I remember something. About Kaitlyn and Maya! And last night when we were playing Russian Spies! I'll bet that is where they were going! That is what they were whispering about that was up in one of those trees! I am about to ask Hayden all about this. But before I can, he is running over to his mom, and they are leaving right away. Geez. What a disaster of a secret teller.

- -

"Me and Addie are prunes," I say to my dad as we walk back to camp. I am wiggling my wrinkly fingers at him. There is a lot of stick, stick, sticky sand in between my toes and all over my flip-flops.

"Yes," my dad says. He seems like maybe he does not want to talk too much. On account of missing his golf game and everything.

"Do not worry," I tell him. "There will be

other days to play golf." That is what my dad always tells me when I want to do something fun like practice gymnastics or hang out with my neighbor Mr. Frisk. But this does not seem to cheer him up.

"We should put away our shovels and buckets," Addie Jokobeck says when we get to the camper. "And then change out of our swimsuits."

This does not sound very fun or funny. But it is the right thing to do. So we put away the shovels and buckets. And then we change out of our swimsuits. I change into a blue tank top with a big pink heart and pink shorts. Addie Jokobeck changes into a tank top and shorts, too. But hers are black. On account of how all her clothes got black.

And then my mom and Kaitlyn and Maya Greenbert are back! And Maya Greenbert's hair is back to being yellow blond!

"Wow," I say. "Your hair is not green anymore."

Maya gives me a mean look. It is one of those looks I know all about. It is a look that means if parents were not around, she would say some mean things to me. But parents are around. So she does not.

The rest of the day is not very fun or funny. That is because my mom thinks we should have some quiet time while my dad finally gets to go play golf. Which means we have to read books and take naps. I like to read books. But I have already read all the very good ones that we have. And I do not like naps, not one little bit.

I try to get Maybelle to do some fun magic, but she does not want to listen. She just wants to lie around and be very sad. On the bright side, we at least get to have a very good campfire that night and make lots of ooey-gooey s'mores that are extremely deli-ciou-so!

The next morning I am up and at 'em very early.

"Good morning!" I yell to everyone. Maya Greenbert throws a pillow at me from her bunk bed. That is not very nice. So I throw it right back. That is called getting what you deserve. "It is time to get up and get to the beach!"

I am very much excited to hear what that

boy Hayden has to say about the disaster area of a tree house.

But my mom makes me go back to sleep. And we do not even get to go to the beach until nine o'clock in the morning! What a very late start to the day.

"I'm scared," Addie Jokobeck says while we are walking right over there. She wanted to bring her cup of baby teeth with her to the beach. But I told her it might get lost. Addie keeps all her baby teeth in one cup, and that is what she holds on to when she gets very nervous in her mind.

"Why are you scared?" I ask. I am looking all around for Maybelle. But she is nowhere to be found. I think she is too sad to go to the beach this morning. On account of Mr. Tuttle maybe taking her magic away.

"Because," Addie whispers so my dad will not hear, "I do not want to go into the woods and have to look at a disaster area of a tree house."

"Do not worry," I tell her. "I will protect you."

But when we get to the beach, we do not even have to worry. Because that boy Hayden is not there! I am upset at first, like maybe I want to have a tantrum. But then I decide to let it go.

"That boy was a big fat liar, anyway," I say. Me and Addie are plopping right down in the sand and making a nice sand castle. The water is very freeze, freeze, freezing on our toes, so we are not going in there, thank you very much. "He did not even know his manners from kindergarten. He might be five even. Not really eight like he said."

"Well, he was very nice when we were playing shark," Addie says. "And he is very good at that game."

"Addie Jokobeck, I am your best friend, not that boy!" I yell. I stand up and throw my shovel right down onto the sand. "Now you take that right back this instant!"

"Of course you are my best friend, Hailey!" Addie says.

"BOO!" someone says right into my ear. And then icy cold water goes rush, rush, rushing

and slide, slide, sliding right around my shoulders and all down my back even.

I scream and turn around. It is that boy, Hayden. He has thrown a big pail of water on me! And now he is running away. And I am getting up and chasing him! But he is very fast! And we go run, run, running all over the beach. And Addie Jokobeck is behind us, running, too. But we are not as fast as Hayden. Probably because he really is in the third grade like he said.

We chase him all the way into the woods. And finally, when we catch him, he is looking up at something. The disaster area of the tree house! It is very scary! It is all falling apart, and it is up in a tree with wood hanging all down and a very high ladder with missing steps!

"Wow," I say. "That really is a disaster area."

"I know," Hayden says. "And there is even a witch that lives up there."

"That is not true!" I say. "There is no witch that lives up there." But I look around just in case. It does seem very spook, spook, spooky. This looks like a very good place for a witch to live.

"Yes, there is," he says. "She is very scary, and she puts spells on people."

"What kind of spells?" I ask. It is too bad Maybelle is not around to hear this. She needs some good lessons about putting spells on people.

"Spells that turn people into monsters and vampires," Hayden says. "And then they have to live in that tree house with her forever."

"Hailey," Addie says. She takes my hand. "I am very scared, and I think we should get out of here now, please."

"Hailey!" my dad yells. I turn around to see him running after us. "What are you doing back here? This is very dangerous. You cannot just go running off like that."

"It's okay," I say. I squeeze Addie Jokobeck's hand. "We were just getting out of here."

"Promise me," he says. "That you will never come back here again."

"I promise," I say.

"I promise," Addie says.

"I promise," Hayden says.

And this time, I do not even cross my fingers behind my back.

- -

Chapter Eight

Maybelle Saves the Day

I did not want to say it, but I am very glad we are getting out of that place. I am very glad we are going back to the beach to play. And guess what? That Hayden is not so mean after all! He is very good at building sand castles! He is very good at making gorgeous windows and doors and towers and all kinds of good things.

"This sand castle reminds me of my own castle," Maybelle says. She came popping right up when we starting building it. "Where I used to live. And I will never be fun, and I will never get my magic back, and I will never go back to living there!" And she sounds very upset about it.

"Yes, you will," I tell her. "Do not worry." I am shoveling some sand into a bucket. Scrape, scrape, scrape. I scrape that sand nice and flat over the top.

"Who are you talking to?" Hayden asks. He is making a very good flag for our sand castle out of a straw that he had in his picnic basket.

"No one," I say real quick.

Maybelle is looking right at our castle. "Your castle would look good with a moat," she says.

"What is a moat?" I whisper real soft. I have never heard of this word *moat*.

"It is water under a drawbridge!" she says. She is getting very excited about this idea. She is even pulling out her wand. This is making me very nervous in my stomach. But I cannot stop her. Because she is not listening to reason. I know all about not listening to reason. It happens to me lots of times, especially when we are having something for dinner that I do not really want to eat.

And then she points her wand at that sand castle. And she tries to make it into a moat! But something goes horribly wrong! And the whole sand castle goes wash, wash, washing away right into the lake.

"Oh, no!" I say.

"Oh, no!" Addie says.

"That's life in the big city," Hayden says. "I guess we will have to start making another one."

But I do not want to start making another one. I want that one! That one that was completely and wonderfully gorgeous and already done! But it is gone. It is washing away all into the water. So I start to get very, very mad. And I start to feel like maybe I am going to have a big tantrum right on this beach.

I do not know what else to do. I am so very upset about that sand castle. I do not want to make a whole other one starting from scratch. I look at Hayden. I look at Addie. I look up to where my dad is sitting under the big umbrella that makes sure his skin does not get all wrinkly in the sun. I stand up and flip my bucket right over, and all the sand in it goes plopping onto the ground. And then I burst into tears.

- -

My dad takes us back to the camper. On account of that I started cry, cry, crying. And on account of that he thinks I am overtired because I was up very early. But I am not even tired one little bit! Which I try to tell him. But he does not listen.

"I am not even tired one little bit," I say.

"I am not either," Addie Jokobeck says.

We are sitting outside our camper at the picnic table. And we are trying to think of something fun to do.

"Hey, Addie," I say. "I know what we could do!"

"What?" She sits up and pays very close attention.

"Well, if we wanted to have a very fun, fun, fun time right now, we could run over to the camper next door and knock on their front door!"

"And then what?" Addie says. "We would try to become friends with them?"

"No."

"We would invite them over for dinner?"

"No."

"We would see if they knew any fun games to play?"

"No," I say. "We would run away and hide!" I cross my arms and wait for her to be very impressed with that idea. But she does not look impressed. Not even one little bit. She just looks confused.

"But why?" she says.

"Like a fun joke," I tell her. "We would run away and hide in those bushes over there. And we would see them come out and say, 'Yoo-hoo, who is knocking on my door, who's there? Yoo-hoo, yoo-hoooo!'"

"That does not sound that fun," Addie Jokobeck says. "That sounds like being naughty."

I do a big sigh. Addie Jokobeck is a very good friend. But she does not get that sometimes being fun and being naughty are the very exact same thing.

Finally it is time for all of us to eat dinner.

My dad pulls out his chef apron. And he puts a lot of hamburgers and hot dogs and pieces of steak right on the grill. And there is a lot of smoke, and when they are done we all sit at the picnic table to eat them, and they taste very good, good, good.

"You should make orange sauce to put on your burger," I tell Addie Jokobeck. Orange sauce is something very tasty that I came up with. It is ketchup and mustard all mixed together. Red ketchup and yellow mustard makes orange sauce! I love orange sauce! It is one of my most favorite foods. You should be allowed to buy it in the grocery store even.

"Okay," Addie Jokobeck says. So we make orange sauce to put on our burgers. And it is very fun and funny and tasty. But Maya and Kaitlyn do not look so happy. On account of the fact that Maya has poison ivy all over her.

And lotion. That she keeps getting on Kaitlyn by accident. And Kaitlyn keeps screaming and saying, "Keep that poison ivy away from me, Maya!"

"Excuse me, Maya," I say. "Would you like me to make you some orange sauce to put on your burger?" I decide that maybe I should try to be nice to her. Since she is very sick with poison ivy and everything. That is called knowing your manners and being polite.

"I am not having a burger," Maya says. "I am having a hot dog."

"Well, that is okay," I say. "You can have orange sauce on a hot dog! You can have orange sauce on anything. Me and Addie can whip you some right up, can't we, Addie?"

"Oh, yes, definitely," Addie says. She is squirting ketchup all over the place. Addie Jokobeck catches on very fast to things. She is a real pro at making orange sauce already. I think she is even maybe going to be a famous chef when she grows up.

"I *said* no thank you," Maya says.

"Kaitlyn?" I try. "Would you like some?"

"No," Maya says. "She doesn't."

"I can answer for myself, Maya," Kaitlyn says. "And I would love some orange sauce." So Addie and I whip up some orange sauce for Kaitlyn. We mix that mustard and ketchup up on a paper plate and then plop it right on her hot dog. *Plop, plop, plop.*

"You will love this orange sauce," Addie tells her.

"Yes," I say. "It is fabulous-o."

"Thank you," Kaitlyn says.

She gives me a big smile. And I give her one right back. I think maybe I will forgive her for being mean to me. I think we might even be sisters again.

- -

After our campfire, I am very sleep, sleep, sleepy. It has been a very long weekend with a visit from Mr. Tuttle and a wrecked sand castle and finding a disaster area of a tree house. I think maybe my mom and dad are very tired, too. On account of how much golf my dad played. And on account of how my mom has been very busy taking Maya to get her hair fixed and helping her put on poison ivy lotion.

So we are all in bed falling asleep after our

campfire. Until I hear some noises that are waking me up! And those noises are Kaitlyn and Maya sneaking right out of the camper! I see them going right out the door.

"Addie," I whisper. "Wake up, wake up, wake up!" I am poke, poke, poking her through her sleeping bag.

"Mmmm," Addie says. She is rolling over and not really waking up even.

"Wake up!" I say again.

"What is going on?" Maybelle whispers. She is on the pillow next to me, and she is rubbing her eyes and looking very sleep, sleep, sleepy.

"Where have you been?" I ask.

"I have been off feeling sorry for myself," she says. She takes a big sniff. Her nose is very red, red, red like maybe she has been crying.

"Well, I was very worried about you," I say. "You missed dinner, and we had orange sauce and everything."

"I love orange sauce!" Maybelle says.

"I know." I try to wake up Addie Jokobeck again, but she is not waking up. So finally I have to give her a small little pinch on her arm.

"Ow!" She rubs her arm. But she is awake! "What'd you do that for?"

"You have to wake up," I tell her. "Kaitlyn and Maya Greenbert have snuck right out of this camper! And we need to find out what they are doing. You know, like Russian Spies." They are probably going down to that witch's tree house. But I do not tell Addie Jokobeck about that. Since she is very afraid of it. And since we promised my dad we would not go back there without even crossing our fingers about it.

"Russian Spies is stupid," Maybelle says. "Everything is a big old disaster of a mess."

I gasp. "It is not stupid!" I say.

"What is not stupid?" Addie Jokobeck asks. Good thing she is still kind of half asleep.

"Oh, nothing," I say. "Just talking to myself."

"I think we should go back to bed," Addie Jokobeck says. She is looking at the clock on the table next to us. The big hand is on the twelve, and the little hand is on the eleven. "The clock says it is eleven o'clock! I am not supposed to be up until eleven o'clock. Only on New Year's. And even then, only if I get a special permission."

"But Kaitlyn and Maya have snuck right out!" I say. "They are gone. So we need to follow them."

I am up and out of bed, and I am putting on my Russian spy clothes of a black sweatshirt and sweatpants. Those clothes will blend in very good with the night, thank you very much.

"Hailey!" Addie whispers. "Please, please, please come back to bed." She is sitting up and looking at me with very frightened eyes.

"It is okay," I tell her. "I know you do not like going out to play Russian Spies. So you stay right in here where it is nice and toasty."

"You can't go out there all by yourself!" Addie says. I am not going to be by my own self. I am going to be with Maybelle. But Addie Jokobeck cannot know that. So she is getting up and out of bed. Because she does not want me to be by myself. That is called being one very true friend.

Addie Jokobeck puts on a black hat and black pants and black shorts and even black sneakers and socks. I do not have any black sneakers or socks. All I have are some purple flip-flops. I do not think Russian spies wear purple flip-flops. But they will have to do.

Then we go sneak, sneak, sneaking out of

the camper. Quiet, quiet, quiet like two little mice. Three little mice if you count Maybelle. But she does not have to be quiet. On account of that no one can hear her anyway.

And then I spot them! Maya and Kaitlyn! They are ahead of us, walking very fast toward the beach.

Addie puts her hand out, and I take it. "Hailey, this is very scary," she says.

"Yes, Hailey," Maybelle says. "This is very scary. And it is not very fun." Maybelle is not even wearing her spy clothes. That is how fast we ran out of there. It is a really good lucky thing that no one can see her.

"I am scared, too," I say. Addie Jokobeck squeezes my hand. We take a few more steps, and then I cannot take it anymore. "I think we should maybe go back to the camper," I say. All of a sudden I am starting to think this might not be the very best idea or plan. It is too dark,

dark, dark out here. And there are mosquitoes that are biting me all up. And maybe even ghosts and vampires and ghouls that are lurking all around this place!

But then something horrible happens. We hear Kaitlyn and Maya say something about how they are going to the tree house. And I know they are talking about that tree house in the back of the woods that is very scary and dangerous and might even have a witch living back there!

"Did you hear that, Addie?" I ask.

"Yes," she says. Her eyes are wide, wide, wide in the dark, like two very big circles. "Hailey, we should go and tell your mom and dad."

"We can't," I say. "It will be too late. We have to follow them and make sure they are okay."

So we go run, run, running after them. But Kaitlyn and Maya have very long legs. And by the time we catch up with them, we are already at the woods! And they are climbing up into that disaster area of a tree house.

"Maya! Kaitlyn!" I yell.

They turn right around. "What are you doing here, Hailey?" Kaitlyn asks. She seems very, very mad at me. I guess she has forgotten all about how nice I was to make her some orange sauce for her hot dog. "You are supposed to be home and in bed!"

"Yes, and so are you," I tell her. I put my hands on my hips. "You cannot go up into that tree house, young lady!"

"Hailey is right," Addie Jokobeck says. "It is not safe, not even one little bit. Your dad even said so!"

"Go home," Kaitlyn hisses. "We are meeting our friends out here."

113

Probably they are meeting some spiky-haired boys. Kaitlyn and Maya are really in love with spiky-haired boys. But spiky-haired boys are not a reason to get into a lot of danger!

"Oh no, oh no, oh no," Maybelle is saying. She is getting very scared about all of this. And I am, too, I must admit. And then Maya starts climbing up the ladder! To the tree house!

"Kaitlyn!" I yell. "Please do not go up there!"

"Hailey," she says. "Go home right this instant!" And then before I know it, she is climbing up there behind Maya.

"Wow," I say. "Those two really do not know how to listen to rules." It is very different to be the one who is trying to get people to listen to rules. Now I know how Addie Jokobeck feels when she is trying to get me to listen to lots and lots of rules. It feels like a very big frustration.

And then something very bad happens. Kaitlyn and Maya are right up in that tree house! And then it starts to shake, shake, shake. And the ladder falls right down!

"Uh-oh," I say.

"Uh-oh," Addie Jokobeck says.

Maya screams. "Ahhhhh!"

I want to tell her that is what she gets for not listening to me. But I do not think this is the time to bring that up.

"Hailey!" Kaitlyn yells. "Push the ladder back up to us so that we can get down immediately!"

"Come on, Hailey," Addie Jokobeck says. She is already over by the ladder trying to pick up that heavy thing.

"I will help you!" I yell. "Hailey Twitch to the rescue!" I grab one end of that ladder. But it is very, very heavy. Two heavy for two seven-year-old girls. But I am not giving up that easy. "Come on, Addie," I say. "Use your strong muscles!"

Addie is using her strong muscles. And I am using my strong muscles. But it is just not enough. That ladder is very much too heavy for us.

"Hailey!" Kaitlyn yells. "Go and get Mom and Dad, quick!"

"Okay," I say. "Me and Addie will go and get them. You two stay up there and do not move a muscle!" Which is a very funny thing to say when you think about it. Since they could not move a muscle even if they wanted to.

Addie and I start to rush, rush, rush right back to the camper to get my mom and dad. Even though now we are all going to be in very big trouble. Like the biggest trouble ever. It is going to be a very bad group of punishments at the Twitch house. *And* the Jokobeck house. And I am definitely going to be called a bad influence.

"Wait a minute," Maybelle says. "I am going to use my magic to make that ladder lighter."

"No," I whisper. "You cannot do that, Maybelle! You are not very good at magic yet." Maybelle might do something that is not helping the situation. Like make the ladder disappear maybe. And then we will be in even worse trouble than we are to begin with.

But Maybelle points her wand right at that
ladder before I can stop her. She waves it all
around, and the ladder lights right up with
sparkles. And then Maybelle says, "Now try to
lift it, Hailey!"

I do not think this is going to work. Because

Maybelle is a very huge disaster with magic.
But I say, "Addie, let's try one more time."

"Hailey, no!" she says. "We have to get your
parents, let's go! Maya is crying." I look up. And
Maya is crying. Big glop, glop, gloppy tears that

are making a very big smudge out of her face. Wow. I guess she is not so tough after all.

"Please, Addie," I say. "I know we can do it this time."

So me and Addie lean down. And we push that ladder! And we pull it! And finally, it goes up!

And Maya and Kaitlyn come down from the tree house.

"Oh my God!" Kaitlyn says. "Thank you so much!"

"Thank you so much!" Maya says. And then they both throw their arms right around me and Addie. We are all hugging and laughing and feeling very relieved in our hearts.

And when I look over, Maybelle is grinning from ear to ear.

Chapter Nine

- - - - - - - - - - - - - - - - - - - -

Time to Go Home

The next morning, we only have a few more hours before it is time to go home. My dad makes us some delicious breakfast sausages on the grill. And my mom makes us all scrambled eggs. And we sit around the picnic table and eat those eggs and spicy sausages right up!

"I think," I tell Addie, "that we should put orange sauce on our eggs!" And I make some up before my mom can see and tell us no, no, no.

"Would you like some orange sauce on your eggs?" I ask Addie.

"Yes, please," she says.

"Would you like some orange sauce on your eggs?" I ask Kaitlyn.

"Yes, please," she says.

"Would you like some orange sauce on your eggs?" I ask Maya Greenbert.

"Yes, please," she says. She gives me a smile.

And later, Maya Greenbert helps me pack up my stuff. And she even gives me one of

her sparkly pink T-shirts that is too small for her now!

So maybe me and her are going to be friends.

– –

When we get home from camp, I am very much exhaustified. It was a very long ride in that car. And then we had to bring Maya home. And Addie home. And Maybelle was driving me crazy since she was so happy about learning to use her magic. She kept singing this song that goes, "I am veryyyy good at maggggic, yes, I ammmm!" It is very stuck in my head now.

I am supposed to be in my room unpacking all of my things. But instead I am trying on the new pink T-shirt Maya gave me and admiring myself right in my mirror.

"Yes," I am saying. "I am the very famous girl who made the stuffed animals come out of that machine. But there are no autographs, thank you very much."

Then Kaitlyn is standing in my doorway.

"Hi, Hails," she says.

"Hello, Kaitlyn," I tell her.

"I just wanted to say thank you for helping us last night." She sits down on my bed. "I'm sorry if Maya and I were mean to you."

"That's okay," I say. "I know that sometimes I can be a pest." It is very true. Sometimes I am a very big pest. Like when Kaitlyn will not let me in her room, and so I knock on the door over and over and over, forever and ever and ever, and I do not go away no matter what.

"You're not a pest," she says, giving me a hug. "You are the best sister ever."

I am feeling very hap, hap, happy. And then Kaitlyn says, "Tomorrow me and Maya are going to the mall. You can come with us if you want."

"Okay!" I say. It has always been my one true dream to go to the mall with Maya and Kaitlyn. They put on makeup and shop for clothes and order orange smoothies, and it seems very fun, fun, fun. I am hoping my mom will let me go and not remember about that punishment she owes me for playing Russian Spies.

"Maybelle!" I say when Kaitlyn is out of the room. "You have done so good! You saved the day—you saved Maya and Kaitlyn!"

"Yay, yay, yay!" Maybelle says. We are jumping up and down, and Maybelle is flying all over. I put my arms out and zoom all around and around the room. "I am a sprite, too!" I say. "I am a flying sprite!"

Then I stand up on my bed and jump right down. But I do not fly, of course. Because I am not a sprite, I am a girl. So I just land on the floor with a big thump.

"Hailey!" my mom yells. "What is going on up there?"

"Nothing!" I say. "Just doing some flying!"

"Flying!" she says. "Well, stop it this instant! And please come down here so that we can talk about your punishment."

Drat.

"I guess we have to go downstairs," I say to Maybelle. That is called facing the music.

But before we can, there is a flash of blue lightning, and Mr. Tuttle pops right up!

"Mr. Tuttle," I say. "You need to get out of here immediately. I am very much late to find out my punishment." But then I have a good idea. "Unless you are so good at magic that you can take away punishments."

"No," Mr. Tuttle says, looking at me through his glasses. "But don't worry, this will not take long." He looks down at his clipboard. "Is it true that Maybelle saved Kaitlyn Twitch and Maya Greenbert from a tree house?"

"Yes!" I say. "It was a very big disaster area of a tree house, and it had a ladder that was very heavy. It was even taller than me," I explain. "And it weighed about three hundred pounds, I think."

"Good," Mr. Tuttle says. He makes a big check mark on his clipboard. "So it is all set," he says. "Maybelle can go back to being a magic sprite."

"Yay!" I say.

"Oh my goodness!" Maybelle says. She is very excited and clapping her hands.

But then Mr. Tuttle says something very horrible. He says, "Are you ready?"

And he holds his hand right out to Maybelle.

"Ready for what?" Maybelle asks.

"Yeah, ready for what?" I ask. This is sounding very suspicious.

"Ready to go back," he says. "Now that you have learned to be fun, and have control of your magic, it is time for you to go back to the castle."

"No!" I say. "Maybelle cannot leave! She can stay here and live here in the Twitch house with her magic."

"Sorry," Mr. Tuttle says. "But those are the rules."

"Says who?" I ask.

"Says the Department of Magic," Mr. Tuttle says.

Hmm. If there is one thing I am not so good with, it is rules. And so I am already coming up with a fab, fab, fabulous plan. A fab, fab, fabulous plan that will get me and Maybelle right out of those rules. A wonderful, perfect plan that will let her stay right here in the Twitch house!

"Excuse me, please," I say to Mr. Tuttle in

my very best polite voice. "But I would like to talk to Maybelle in private."

I pull Maybelle right out into the hallway. And then I start to whisper my plan right into her ear...

Acknowledgments

Thank you so, so, so much to:

My awesome agent, Alyssa Henkin

My editor, Rebecca Frazer

Everyone at Sourcebooks for all their support, including Dominique Raccah, Kelly Barrales-Saylor, Kay Mitchell, Kristin Zelazko, and Aubrey Poole

My mom and dad

My sisters, Krissi and Kelsey

My BFFs, Kevin Cregg and Scott Neumyer

About the Author

Lauren Barnholdt loves reading, writing, and anything pink and sparkly. She's never had a magic sprite, but she does have four guinea pigs. She lives outside Boston with her husband. Visit her website and say hello at www.laurenbarnholdt.com.

About the Illustrator

Suzanne Beaky grew up in Gahanna, Ohio, and studied illustration at Columbus College of Art and Design. Her expressive illustrations are commissioned by children's book, magazine, and educational publishers worldwide. She and her husband live in Kirksville, Missouri, with their cats who insist on sitting in her lap while she works and often step in her paint.